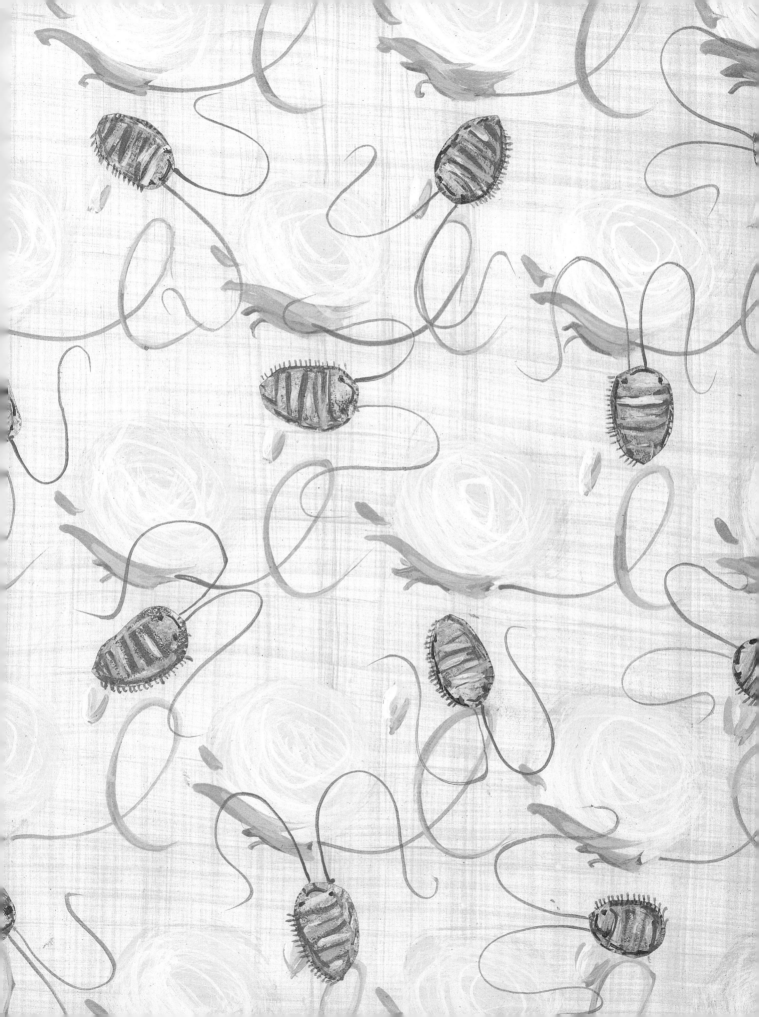

For Claudia Maoly – J.D.
For Andrew, Otto & Jim – K.G.

First published 2010 by Macmillan Children's Books
a division of Macmillan Publishers Limited
20 New Wharf Road, London N1 9RR
Basingstoke and Oxford
Associated companies throughout the world
www.panmacmillan.com

ISBN: 978-0-330-51118-6

Text copyright © Julia Donaldson 2010
Illustrations copyright © Karen George 2010
Moral rights asserted.

11 13 15 14 12 10

A CIP catalogue record for this book is available from the British Library.

Printed in China

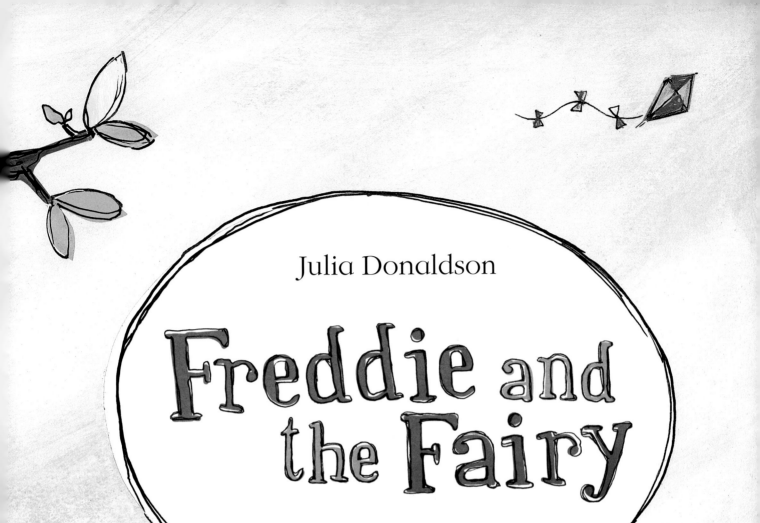

Julia Donaldson

Freddie and the Fairy

Karen George

MACMILLAN CHILDREN'S BOOKS

Freddie found a fairy
Tangled in a tree.
"Help! I'm stuck!" the fairy cried,
So Freddie set her free.

"Thank you," said the fairy.
"My name is Bessie-Belle.
I'll grant you all your wishes,
Though I can't hear very well."

Freddie thought, then mumbled:
"I wish I had a pet."

"Why, so you shall!" said Bessie-Belle,
And conjured up . . .

. . . a net.

"I don't want *fish*," said Freddie.

"I'd rather have a dog."
"Hey presto!" said the fairy,
And conjured up . . .

. . . a frog.

"Let's try again," said Freddie.
"I wish I had a cat."
"That's easy!" said the fairy,
And conjured up . . .

. . . a bat.

"I don't like bats," said Freddie,

"But what about a mouse?"

"Lift up that stone!" the fairy said,

And Freddie found . . .

. . . a louse.

"That isn't right!" said Freddie.
"Let's think. Perhaps a parrot?"

"I'll do my best," said Bessie-Belle,
And conjured up . . .

. . . a carrot.

Freddie stamped his foot and said,
"This carrot has no beak."
"Forgive me," said the fairy
And a tear rolled down her cheek.

Just then, from out of nowhere,
Appeared the Fairy Queen.
She dried the fairy's eyes, and asked,
"Whatever does this mean?"

"It's Bessie-Belle," said Freddie.
"She gets things wrong," he grumbled.
"I'm sorry," said the fairy,
"But that's because you mumbled."

"Now, Freddie," said the Fairy Queen.
(She sounded kind but stern.)
"Before you wish again, there are
Three rules for you to learn.

no!

by order F.Q.

no!

by order F.

"Rule One: you mustn't mumble.
Rule Two: don't turn away.
The fairy needs to see your lips
To read the words you say.

Rule Three: don't cover up your mouth.
She can't see through your hand!
Obey these three gold rules, and then
I'm sure she'll understand."

So Freddie learnt the three gold rules
And now he speaks quite clearly,

And everything he
wishes for comes true –

or very nearly.